Stories for 3 Year Olds

Stories for Year Olds 3

tiger tales

Contents

Little Bear's Big Sweater   7
David Bedford & Caroline Pedler

Fun in the Sun – Poems   36

"From a Railway Carriage"
Robert Louis Stevenson

"Long Beach Days"

"Sunny Day"

Pirate Piggy Wiggy   39
Diane & Christyan Fox

In the Garden – Poems   60

"Caterpillar"
Christina Rossetti

"Have You Watched the Fairies?"
Rose Fyleman

"The Ladybug"

"Butterfly"

The Busy, Busy Day   63
Claire Freedman & Daniel Howarth

Happy Time – Poems   90

"Happy Thoughts"
Robert Louis Stevenson

"Party Treats"

"Happy Days"

It's My Turn!   93
David Bedford & Elaine Field

Silly Time – Poems   120

"If a Pig Wore a Wig"
Christina Rossetti

"The Snake and the Mittens"

"Anna Elise"

A Friend Like You   123
Julia Hubery & Caroline Pedler

When the Stars Come   150
Out – Poems

"Stars on High"

"Good Night!"
Victor Hugo

"Night"
William Blake

By the Light of the   153
Silvery Moon
Claire Freedman & Stephen Gulbis

Little Bear's Big Sweater

by David Bedford   *Illustrated by* Caroline Pedler

Big Bear loved his striped sweater.
It was warm. It was soft. And it
was his very favorite.

But it was getting harder and
harder to wear.

"It's too small for you!" said
Little Bear, giggling.

"It's not," said Big Bear.
"It fits just right!"

Mom laughed. "I think it's time I knitted you a new sweater, Big Bear. Why don't you give that one to your brother?"

"But it's too big for him," said Big Bear.
"No, it's not," said Little Bear.

He pulled it quickly over his head.
"It fits just right!"

"You'd better take care of it,"
said Big Bear. "It's my
favorite sweater—EVER."

"I will," said Little Bear,
happily. "It's my favorite
ever, too!"

Together, they ran off
to play. "Now I look just
like you!" cried Little Bear.

Big Bear gave his brother a piggyback ride
through the tall grass. Little Bear
chuckled as he was jiggled around.

The two brothers jumped
through the puddles with a
Splish! Splash! Splosh!
"This is fun!" said Big Bear.

Then Big Bear
climbed along a
high branch.
"I'm climbing too!"
said Little Bear.
"You're pulling
me down,"
cried his brother.

"I can wibble-wobble like you!" said Little Bear.

"Stop it!" said Big Bear. "You're wobbling
too much!"

And suddenly . . .

Crack! went the log,
as it split in two.
Sploosh!

went the bears as they landed
in a muddy puddle.

"Look what you've done!" yelled
Big Bear. "You've broken the
wobbly log. And you've
ruined MY sweater!"

Little Bear looked down at
the soggy sweater. His lip
began to tremble.

"I'm s-o-r-r-y!" he said,
and he ran away into the
woods.

"Well, good," said Big Bear,
grumpily. "It's better playing
on my own."

Big Bear slid down the slippery-slidey
slope. He chased a butterfly until
he was dizzy. Then he sat on
the end of the see-saw.
But with only one
bear, it wouldn't
go up or down.

*Playing is no fun
without Little Bear, he
thought. And he began to
feel very lonely.*

*Where ARE you,
Little Bear?*

Big Bear searched
the places Little Bear
liked the most. He
looked everywhere.
But he wasn't
in the hollow
honey tree . . .

or in their den
in the bush . . . .

He wasn't even hiding under
the big rock.
Little Bear wasn't anywhere!
Where could he have
gone, all on
his own?

Suddenly, Big Bear saw a
woolly thread. So he followed it
quickly through the trees, around
a bush, and deeper and deeper into
the woods, until at last
he found . . .

a very sad and
lonely Little Bear.

"I've ruined our favorite
ever sweater!" Little Bear
cried when he saw him.

29

Big Bear gave his brother a big hug.

"Don't worry," he said, kindly.
"It's only a sweater! I'm sorry
I yelled at you."

"It's all right,"
Little Bear
sniffed. "I
shouldn't have
run off."

Big Bear
took him by
the hand. "Let's
go home,"
he said.

On the way back,
Big Bear wrapped
up all the wool
into a ball.

"We had a little accident,"
he told Mom when they
got home.
"Poor Little Bear!"
said Mom. "Don't worry—
I know just what to do."

The very next morning,
Big Bear and Little Bear
had the best surprise . . .
two brand-new, matching,
striped sweaters!

"Now I can be just like
you, Little Bear!" said
Big Bear. "You're the best
brother EVER!"

Fun in the Sun

From a Railway Carriage

Faster than fairies, faster than witches,

Bridges and houses, hedges and ditches;

And charging along like troops in a battle

All through the meadows the horses and cattle:

All of the sights of the hill and the plain

Fly as thick as driving rain;

And ever again, in the wink of an eye,

Painted stations whistle by.

~ Robert Louis Stevenson

Long Beach Days

Pat a sandcastle,
Find a seashell.
Stick in a flag,
And some seaweed as well.

Quick! Grab the bucket
Race to the sea
Up to my knees now
Yay—look at me!

Sunny Day

Hip-hooray,
A sunny day!
Skip outside—
It's time to play!

Pirate PiggyWiggy

by Diane and Christyan Fox

Sometimes when I
sail my little boats,
I dream of what it
might be like to be a
brave pirate!

"Arrgh!"

I would wear
a big black hat,
a patch over my eye,
and have a parrot
on my shoulder . . . .

My ship would be the finest that ever sailed the seven seas.

At nighttime, we could sit around the fire singing pirate songs....

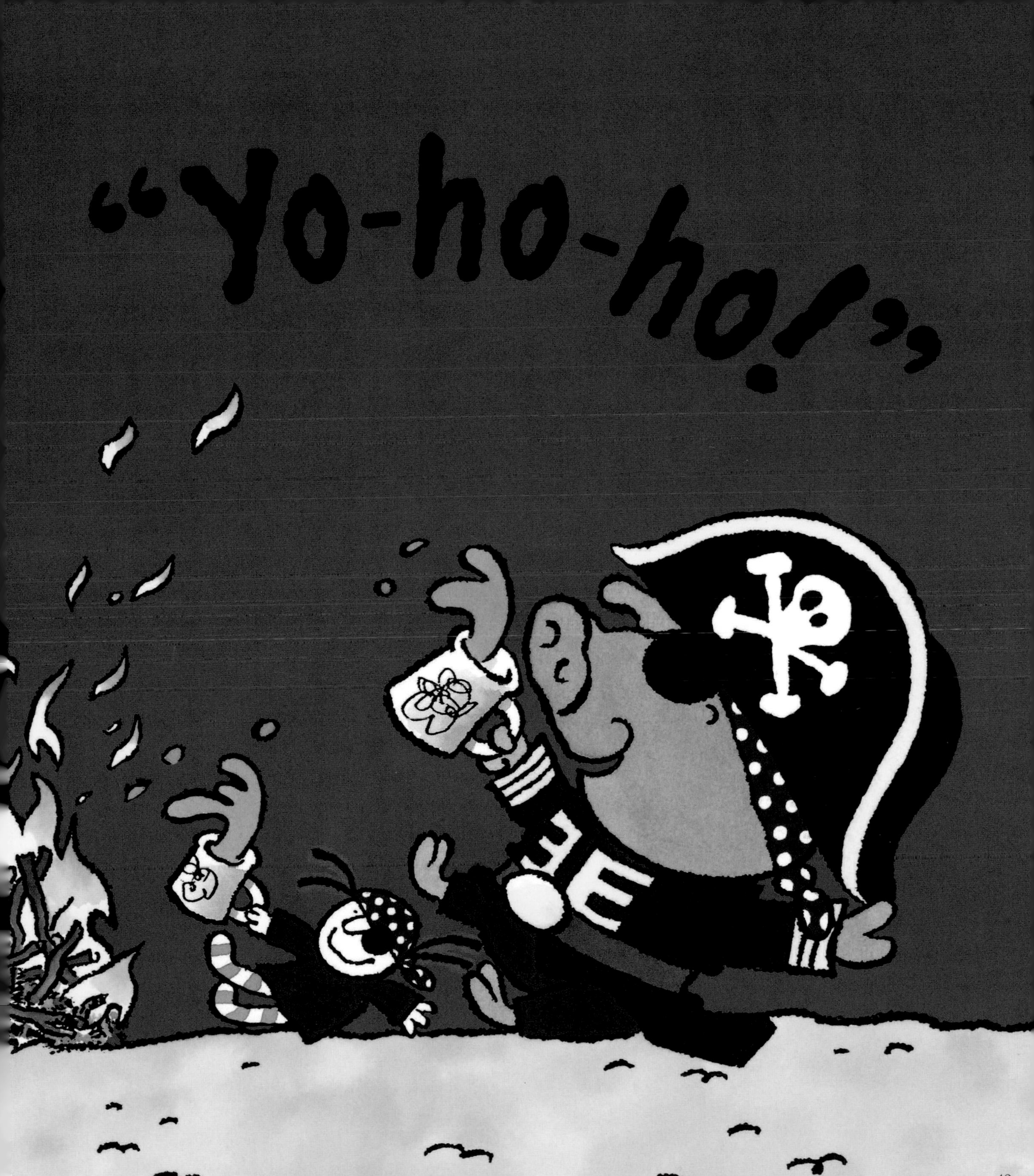
"Yo-ho-ho!"

On Crossbone Island we would search for treasure.

Ten paces north . . .
eight paces south . . . .

Shiver me Timbers, "X" marks the spot!

The richest treasure ever seen . . . .

But we'd have to
sail back home again

to find the treasure
we love best!

In the Garden

Caterpillar

Brown and furry
Caterpillar in a hurry,
Take your walk
To the shady leaf, or stalk,
Or what not,
Which may be the chosen spot.

~ Christina Rossetti

Have You Watched the Fairies?

Have you watched the fairies
when the rain is done
Spreading out their little wings
to dry them in the sun?
I have, I have! Isn't it fun?

~ Rose Fyleman

The Ladybug

Some lucky ladybugs have six big black spots,
And some little ones just have four.
Sometimes I count spots—
One, two, three, STOP! STOP!
See it fly off before I can count any more!

Butterfly

Butterflies dance in butterfly sky.
Butterflies swoop and spin when they fly.
Butterflies drift and butterflies roam.
Flutter on, butterflies—all the way home!

The Busy, Busy Day

by Claire Freedman   Illustrated by Daniel Howarth

"Hooray! Spring is here!" cried Ginger, tugging on his old boots. "Come on, Floppy, let's go do some gardening."

They dashed outside and looked around.

"What should we do first, Ginger?" asked Floppy excitedly.

"I know!" said Ginger. "Let's clear away those logs."
And he went to get the wheelbarrow.

CHIRP!   CHIRP!   CHIRP!

Two worried-looking robins swooped down.
"Hmmm, something's bothering them," said
Ginger. "I can't see anything wrong, can you?"

"No!" said Floppy, shaking his head. "Maybe
they think we want to eat their worms!"

They looked in the wheelbarrow and couldn't believe their eyes. Snug in one corner lay a nestful of baby robins!

CHEEP! CHEEP! CHEEP!

"So that's why the robins were chirping," said Ginger. "They thought we might scare their baby chicks. We'd better not disturb them."

"What should we do now, Ginger?" Floppy asked.

"Hmm," said Ginger thoughtfully. "Well, we can't clear away the logs without a wheelbarrow. Let's do something else instead."

They started to pick up the flowerpots and stack them.

"Come look at this, Floppy," Ginger whispered. "I've found something else! But be very, very quiet!"

Inside the biggest flowerpot, two tiny hedgehogs were curled up, fast asleep. They snuffled and snored noisily.

"Oooh!" gasped Floppy excitedly. "They look so funny!"

"Shhh, don't say a word!" Ginger hushed. "We don't want to wake them!"

They both tiptoed away without a sound.

"Well, Floppy," said Ginger. "We can't clean up the flowerpots. But we can clean up the shed." And he opened the shed door.

EEEK! EEEK! EEEK!

"That's not the door creaking," said Ginger. "Is it you making that funny noise, Floppy?"

"No!" Floppy giggled. "Maybe your old boots are squeaking, Ginger."

"It's not me *or* my boots," Ginger replied. "So what can it be?"

Floppy peered along the dusty shelves
between the boxes and baskets.

"Achoo!" he sneezed.

Ginger checked the bulb packets. Floppy
tipped the watering can upside-down.

Nothing!

EEEK! EEEK!

"There it is again, Floppy!" said Ginger.
"What is it?"

"I don't know," said Floppy. "But it's a
very loud squeak!"

Ginger sat down by some seed trays to
think . . . and almost squashed a family
of mice!

"Wow, that was close!" said Ginger. "So
that's what was squeaking! Well, we can't
clean out the shed now. We might disturb
the mice!"

Ginger closed the shed door quietly behind them. "Don't worry, Floppy!" he said. "We can still do the weeding."

Floppy kneeled beside the flowerbeds. A big orange butterfly landed on his nose.

"Hee hee!" laughed Floppy. "That tickles!"

"Aha!" Ginger said to Floppy. "I think the butterflies are trying to tell us something!"

"What could *that* be?" asked Floppy in surprise.

Ginger looked closely at the dandelion leaves.

"Just as I thought," he said. "Caterpillars!

One day they'll grow into butterflies, too.

No more weeding 'til then!"

Ginger and Floppy walked back up to the garden, and Ginger pulled off his old boots.

"Our garden may not be neat," he said, looking around, "but I think it's perfect just the way it is!"

"You're right, Ginger," Floppy agreed happily. "It's perfect for all of our friends and . . ."

". . . it's just perfect for a sunny picnic, too!"

Ginger got the picnic blanket. Floppy
brought out some orangeade and cupcakes.

"Everyone can enjoy our garden," Ginger
said cheerfully as they started to eat.

And everyone did!

Happy Time

Happy Thoughts

The world is so full of a number of things,
I'm sure we should all be as happy as kings.

~ Robert Louis Stevenson

Party Treats

Ice cream in my tum-tum,
Squishy cake galore.
Sweet and gooey fun-fun—
Can I have some more?

Happy Days

On rainy days, I play outside.

I splash in puddles—slip and slide!

On sunny days, I'm in the sea,

With water splashing at my knee.

On windy days, I race and swoop.

Just like a plane—I loop-the-loop!

On snowy days, I wear my hat,

And scoop up snowballs—squish, squash, SPLAT!

Oh, what a lot of games I've found,

In every weather, all year 'round!

It's My Turn!

by David Bedford   Illustrated by Elaine Field

Playground

Oscar and Tilly found a playground.

"Let's play on the slide," said Oscar.

"I'll go first," said Tilly.

"I'll slide now," said Oscar.

"Not yet," said Tilly.

"It's not your turn."

"That looks fun,"
said Oscar. "Is it
my turn now?"
"Not yet," said Tilly.

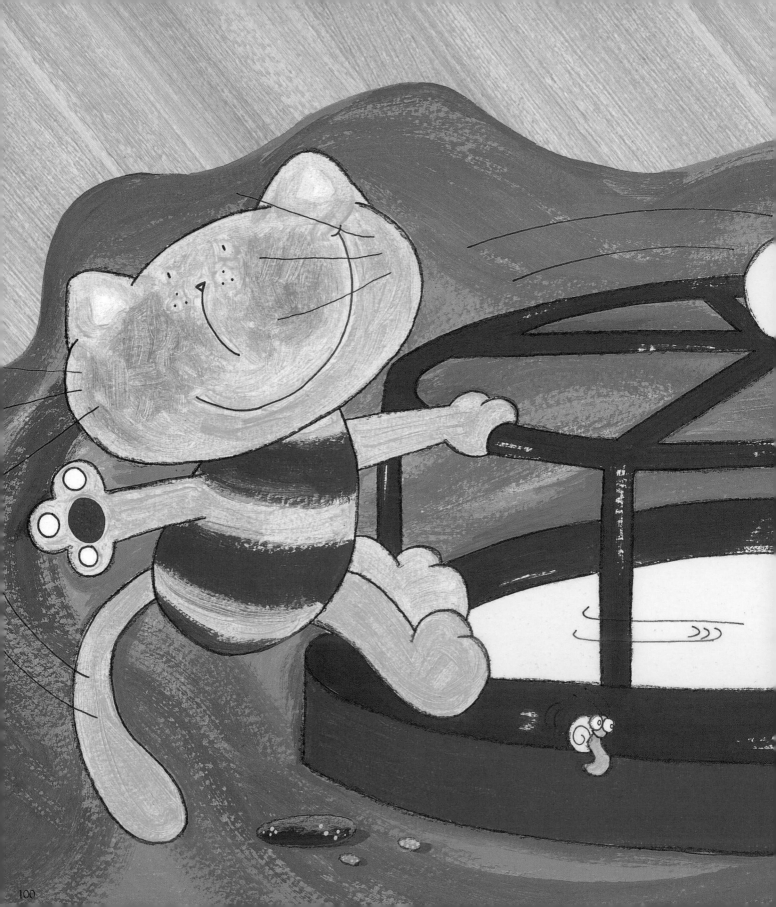

Tilly went around and
around on the merry-go-round.
"Is it my turn yet?" asked Oscar.
"No," said Tilly. "I'm not finished."

Tilly went around

and around

and around

and AROUND . . . .

"I feel dizzy," said Tilly.

"Hee, hee," cried Oscar. "It's my turn now—you're too wobbly!"

"This is fun."

"I feel better now," said Tilly.

"Can I slide after you?"

"No," said Oscar. "It's not your turn."

"Can I play on the swing after you?" asked Tilly.
"No," said Oscar. "It's still my turn."

"Get off, Tilly," shouted Oscar.
"It's my turn on the see-saw."
"The see-saw doesn't work," said Tilly.
But when Oscar jumped on the other end . . .

... Tilly went up in the air!

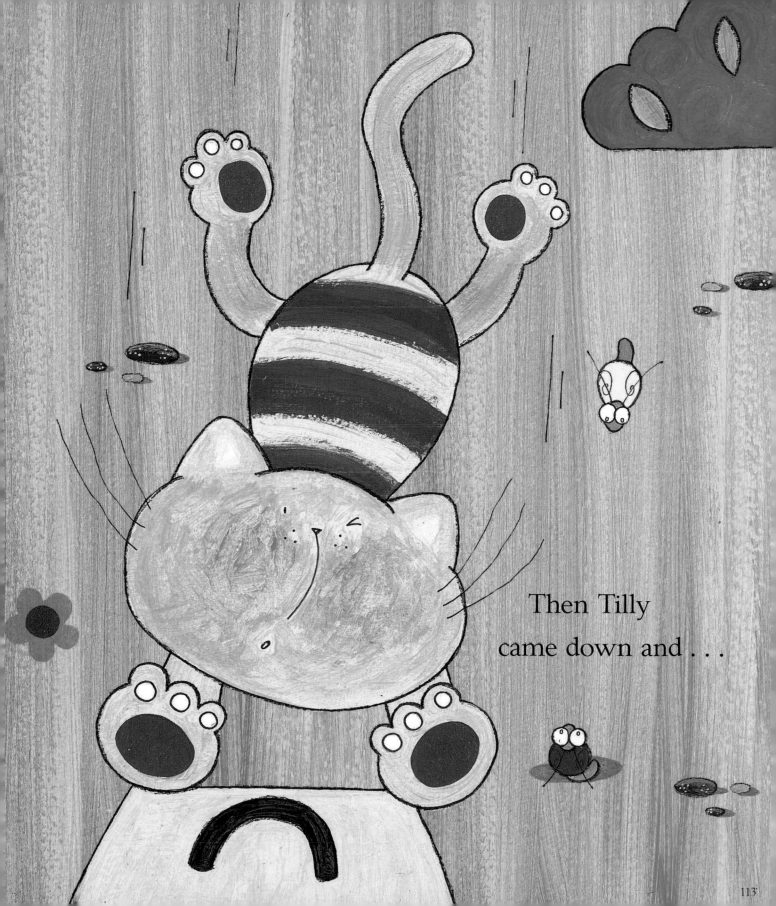

Then Tilly
came down and . . .

Oscar went up . . .

WHOO

and then . . .

Oscar and Tilly played
together all afternoon.

Silly Time

If a Pig Wore a Wig

If a pig wore a wig,
What could we say?
Treat him as a gentleman,
And say "Good day."

~ Christina Rossetti

The Snake and the Mittens

I fear I made a dreadful mistake,
When I knitted mittens for a snake.
He said, "'Twas kind of you to knit,
But I just don't think they'll ever fit."

Anna Elise

Anna Elise, she jumped with surprise;

The surprise was so quick, it played her a trick;

The trick was so rare, she jumped in a chair;

The chair was so frail, she jumped in a pail;

The pail was so wet, she jumped in a net;

The net was so small, she jumped on a ball;

The ball was so round, she jumped on the ground;

And ever since then she's been turning around.

A Friend Like You

by Julia Hubery

Illustrated by
Caroline Pedler

Panda stretched happily in the
morning sun. It was the first day
of spring, time for his special
journey up into the mountains.

Sunlight sparkled in the trees as Panda walked through the peaceful forest. Suddenly, a nut hit him on the nose. It was Monkey!

"Where are you going, Panda?" he giggled. "Anywhere fun?"

"Somewhere with a beautiful
secret," said Panda. "Do you want
to come, too?"

"Yes, please!" squealed Monkey.
"I love secrets!"

As they set off, Monkey danced around Panda, hurrying him along. "Come on," he squeaked. "I want to see the secret!"

"Slow down, little friend," said Panda. "It's a long way. We have to cross Silver River first, then follow the rocky stream to the mountain meadows."

"That sounds easy," said Monkey. "Let's get going, Panda-plod!" And he raced ahead.

Panda padded on in the leafy shade. As he stopped to chew some bamboo, he heard chirping under the leaves. There he found a beautiful bird, bright as a jewel.

"Monkey, come see this!" he called.

But Monkey was out of sight.

Poor Monkey, thought Panda.

In such a rush, he never sees anything!

I wonder where he went?

Before long, Panda
found him chasing
his tail around a tree.
"You're taking forever," said Monkey,
"and I can't find the silly river!"
"If you hush for a minute, you'll hear
it," said Panda. "We're almost there."

"But I'm too excited to hush!" laughed Monkey, chattering away as they strolled on together.

Soon they reached
the banks of Silver River.
"I'm going to swing across," boasted
Monkey. "Watch me fly, Panda!"
"Be careful!" Panda called out, as Monkey
leaped up into the branches.
Panda swam slowly down into the cool
water, smiling as a shoal of flickering fish
tickled by his toes.

Monkey came swinging
through the treetops.
"I'll beat you across,
old soggy-ploddy-bear!"
he shouted.

One,
two,
three,
Whheeeeee
look at
Meeeeee!

Monkey let go of his branch,
and soared up, up through
the glorious sky . . .

. . . then down, **Splash!** into the river.

"Help!" he shrieked.

"Here I am!" shouted Panda. "Hold on tight!"

He pulled the shivering monkey from the water and swam to the shore.

"Poor little monkey-mess! How did I ever
find a friend like you?" Panda laughed.
"Come on—you can ride on my back!"
Monkey snuggled into Panda's cozy fur.
"Thank you, Panda," he whispered.

Up and up Panda climbed through the misty foothills.

"Monkey, did you ever see anything so pretty?" he gasped, but there was no answer. Monkey was fast asleep.

"Sleep well, little friend," Panda whispered, and padded softly on.

At last, they reached the lush, green meadows.
"Are we there?" squeaked Monkey,
bouncing awake. "Can I see the secret now?"
"It's up in the highest meadow," said Panda.
"The mountain butterflies are about to fly—
it's an amazing sight!"

"Quick, I want to see them!" Monkey squealed.

"Wait!" called Panda. "I can't keep up."

"But they'll fly away!" Monkey cried, skipping off. Panda sighed sadly and climbed slowly after him.

When Panda reached the top, Monkey was looking very upset. "There aren't any butterflies!" he snapped. "We've missed them, all because you're such a slowpoke!"

"That's not very fair," cried Panda. "I can't rush like you. It's just the way I am."

Monkey hung his head. "I'm sorry, Panda," he said.
"I know I'm lucky to have a friend like you."

Panda smiled. "Don't worry, little Monkey,"
he said gently. "All we have to do now is wait quietly."

Monkey snuggled next to Panda,
and slowly, slowly, slowly . . .

. . . a thousand butterflies stretched their wings
and flew into the air.

"They're amazing!" Monkey whispered.
"Thank you, Panda."

Panda hugged him and smiled. "I'm happy that
I can share them with a friend like you."

When the Stars Come Out

Stars on High

One, two—stars on high,

Three, four—in the sky,

Five, six—burning bright,

Seven, eight—in the night,

Nine, ten—I declare,

Too many stars to count up there!

Good Night!

Good night! Good night!
Far flies the light.
But still God's love,
Shall flame above,
Making all bright.
Good night!

~ Victor Hugo

Night

The sun descending in the west
The evening star does shine,
The birds are silent in their nest
And I must seek for mine.

~ William Blake

By the Light of the
Silvery Moon

by Claire Freedman

Illustrated by Steve Gulbis

Down on the farm,
the moon is up,
And nighttime
is starting to fall.
But Little Gray Hare
is wide awake;
He's not feeling
sleepy at all.

"Look at the moon!"
cries Little Gray Hare.
"Mommy, it's shining
so bright!
"Let's play!" he calls to the
woolly white lambs,
And they scamper off
into the night.

White moonbeams dance
on the henhouse roof.
The chicks should be
curled up asleep.
But out they all tumble,
one by one.
"Let's go and explore,"
they cheep.

Tucked in their sty,
the piglets can't sleep.
"Let's play a game!"
they say.
A shooting star
streaks past the moon
As they romp in the
sweet, fresh hay.

Little Hare hops
to the moonlit pond.
The ducklings
are splashing about.
"Back to the nest,"
Mommy Duck quacks.
"But we want to play
games!" they shout.

"It's sleepy-time now!"
Mommy Cat calls.
She searches each
hiding place.
"But we're not ready!"
the kittens meow,
And out of the barnyard
they race.

It's very late now,
and everyone's tired.
It's bedtime for
small sleepyheads!
So yawning and sighing,
away they all creep,
Back home to their
cozy, warm beds.

Last one asleep
is Little Gray Hare,
So snug on the soft,
mossy floor.
"Hush!" sighs his mommy,
"Sleep tight," smiles the moon,
And the only sound now
is a snore!

STORIES FOR 3 YEAR OLDS

tiger tales

5 River Road, Suite 128, Wilton, CT 06897
Published in the United States 2014
First published in Great Britain 2013
by Little Tiger Press
This volume copyright © 2013 Little Tiger Press
Cover artwork by Rachel Baines
Cover artwork copyright © 2010, 2013 Little Tiger Press
ISBN-13: 978-1-58925-521-0
ISBN-10: 1-58925-521-6
Printed in China
LTP/1800/1852/0317

For more insight and activities,
visit us at www.tigertalesbooks.com

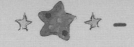

LITTLE BEAR'S BIG SWEATER

by David Bedford
Illustrated by Caroline Pedler

First published in Great Britain 2008
by Little Tiger Press, London

PIRATE PIGGY WIGGY

by Diane and Christyan Fox

First published in Great Britain 2003
by Little Tiger Press, London

THE BUSY, BUSY DAY

by Claire Freedman
Illustrated by Daniel Howarth

First published in Great Britain 2004
by Little Tiger Press, London

ACKNOWLEDGEMENTS

"Stars on High" by Stephanie Stansbie, copyright © 2008 Little Tiger Press;
"Long Beach Days," "Butterfly," "Party Treats," "Happy Days" by Stephanie Stansbie,
copyright © 2013 Little Tiger Press;
"Sunny Day," "The Ladybug," "The Snake and the Mittens" by Mara Alperin,
copyright © 2013 Little Tiger Press

Additional artwork by Rachel Baines, copyright © 2010, 2013 Little Tiger Press

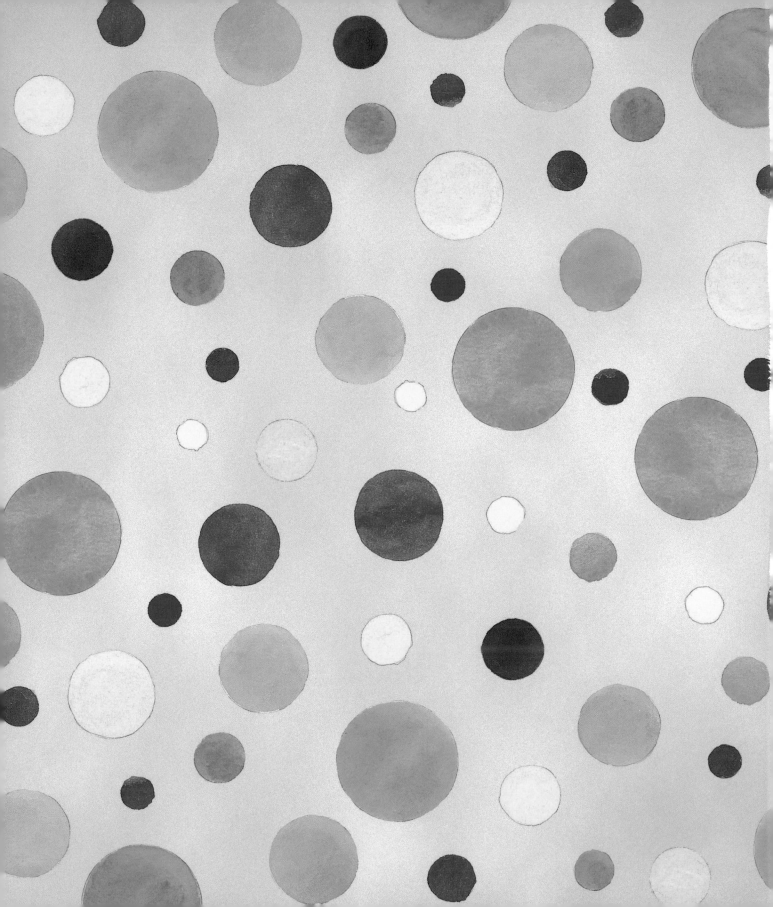